You find a drainpipe that leads from the gutters at your feet to somewhere down below. You reach down and shake the pipe. It seems solid enough. You carefully climb down to the roof below. Now you have only two stories to go. Unfortunately, the drainpipe ends right there.

Nearby, the high, sharply pitched roof of a smaller building next door is only a couple of feet away. You jump over and slide down the slates, coming to a stop at the gutter along the bottom of the roof.

Just below you is a line of clothes washing—bloomers, nightdresses, and sheets.

You jump off into midair, grabbing the sheets on the line and swinging in an arc as they come loose. This breaks your fall a bit, but you land heavily on the roof of a dog house. You look around, then jump off the side and down to the ground.

At the same moment, a large dog comes charging out, its teeth clashing after you and growling in anger. What will you do?

ONLY *YOU*, AS YOUNG INDIANA JONES, CAN DECIDE...

Bantam Books in the Choose Your Own Adventure® series
Ask your bookseller for the books you have missed

THE YOUNG INDIANA JONES CHRONICLES™

Book 4

MASTERS OF THE LOUVRE

PARIS, July 1908

By Richard Brightfield

Adapted from the television episode
"Paris, July 1908"
Teleplay by Reg Gadney
Story by George Lucas

Illustrated by Frank Bolle

BANTAM BOOKS
NEW YORK · TORONTO · LONDON · SYDNEY · AUCKLAND

RL 5, age 10 and up

MASTERS OF THE LOUVRE
A Bantam Book / January 1993

CHOOSE YOUR OWN ADVENTURE® *is a registered trademark of
Bantam Books, a division of Bantam Doubleday
Dell Publishing Group, Inc.
Registered in U.S. Patent and Trademark Office and elsewhere.
Original concept of Edward Packard*

THE YOUNG INDIANA JONES CHRONICLES™
*is a trademark of Lucasfilm Ltd.
All rights reserved. Used under authorization.*

*Cover art by George Tsui
Interior illustrations by Frank Bolle*

ISBN 0-553-29969-7

Published simultaneously in the United States and Canada

*Bantam Books are published by Bantam Books, a division of Bantam
Doubleday Dell Publishing Group, Inc. Its trademark, consisting of the
words "Bantam Books" and the portrayal of a rooster, is Registered
in U.S. Patent and Trademark Office and in other countries. Marca
Registrada. Bantam Books, 666 Fifth Avenue, New York, New York
10103.*

PRINTED IN THE UNITED STATES OF AMERICA

OPM   0   9   8   7   6   5   4   3   2   1

MASTERS OF
THE LOUVRE

Your Adventure

The year is 1908. You are young Indiana Jones, the son of a professor of medieval studies at Princeton University in New Jersey. In this book you are traveling through Paris with your parents, Professor Henry and Anna Jones, and your tutor, Miss Helen Seymour.

In the adventures that follow, you will get to meet many famous figures in history, such as Norman Rockwell and Pablo Picasso. You will also experience life in Paris and learn about the various art movements of the time. You may even be on hand for a party honoring the famous artist Henri Rousseau and become involved in an elaborate scheme involving a forged painting.

From time to time as you read along, you will be asked to make a choice. The adventures you have as Indiana Jones are the results of your choices. You are responsible because you choose. After you make your decision, follow the instructions to find out what happens to you next. Remember, your adventures in Paris depend on the actions you decide to take.

To help you in your travels, a special glossary is provided at the end of the book.

You are Indiana Jones. You were born on July 1, 1899 in Princeton, New Jersey, where your father is a professor of medieval studies at the university. It is now 1908, and you are nine years old. You are traveling around the world with your mother and father. With you is your tutor, Miss Helen Seymour.

You are on a train traveling east across the French countryside heading toward Paris. Miss Seymour has the seat next to you, and your parents are seated behind you. You are looking out the window. Every once in a while, the train rushes by one of the small, tidy French villages. The houses have steeply pitched slate roofs punctuated with many brick chimneys. Almost always there is a large medieval church at the center of the village.

"This trip should give you a good chance to polish your French," Miss Seymour says. "The French are very sensitive to correct grammar and pronunciation. I hope you don't disgrace me with your accent."

→ → → → → → → → → → → → →

Turn to page 2.

"I'll try not to," you say in your best French, wishing you could just speak plain English for a change.

"We'll tour the galleries, especially the Louvre, and see some of the world's finest masterpieces of art," Miss Seymour goes on. "It will definitely broaden your education."

You groan inwardly. Now you *know* you're not going to enjoy this trip. It's just going to be study, study, and even more study—as usual. And all the time under the ever-watchful eye of Miss Seymour. You hope that somewhere along the line you'll be able to sneak off and see some of the *really* interesting sights of Paris that you've read about.

Then, almost as if she were reading your thoughts, Miss Seymour says, "Of course there will be times when you will be left more or less on your own. Your parents are going off to the south of France, and I need to catch up on my correspondence. I have many letters to write and send off."

I can hardly wait, you say to yourself, settling back into your seat.

As the train chugs into the suburbs of the city, the towers of Paris appear in the distance. You are now speeding along the banks of a wide river.

"That's the Seine," Miss Seymour says. "It divides Paris in two. They call this side the Left

Bank and the other side the Right Bank. The two are connected by many bridges. In the Middle Ages the original city of Paris was on an island in the river called the Île de la Cité, on which the Cathedral of Notre-Dame is located. The city we now know as Paris grew up on the banks on both sides."

Finally the train pulls into a cavernous railroad station and hisses to a stop, the smoke from the locomotive billowing up toward the high, vaulted ceiling.

"This is the Gare d'Orsay on the Left Bank, where we get off," your father says, coming up the aisle. "We have arrived."

You grab your bags from the overhead rack and follow your parents and Miss Seymour off the train. They lead you to the part of the station where taxis are lined up waiting for passengers. The taxis look like they could be horse-drawn carriages, except there are motors in front instead of horses.

4

The four of you climb into the enclosed cab of one of the taxis while a porter loads your bags on a rack in the back. The driver climbs into the open-air seat in front.

You leave the station and pull out into city traffic. Most of the other vehicles, like passenger carriages and wagons, are still horse drawn. Double-decker buses, with a stairway in back going up to the top level, are drawn by a team of two horses. But there are also a few other motor-driven taxis besides your own, and you even pass an electric streetcar.

Your father calls out the address of your hotel on the Boulevard St. Germain to the driver.

"Is that where we stayed the last time we were in Paris?" your mother asks.

"No, that was on the Right Bank near the Champs-Élysées," your father says. "This hotel is much smaller, but I think you'll find it very cozy."

"And the hotel will be a nice, quiet place to study," Miss Seymour adds.

Oh, great, you think to yourself. Here you are in Paris, and all she can think about is studying.

Your parents see the look on your face.

"Miss Seymour will take you to all the famous sights, like the Eiffel Tower and Notre-Dame," your mother says.

"And the Louvre," Miss Seymour adds.

→ → → → → → → → → → → →

Turn to page 6.

"We'll all go to the Louvre for a start," your father says. "Even when I have only a short time in Paris, I never miss going there."

The taxi pulls up in front of the hotel. The manager, a short, stocky woman with graying hair tied in a bun, comes out to supervise the unloading of your bags. She looks very serious.

"This is Madame Lili, the concierge of the hotel," your father says, introducing you.

"You are in luck," Lili says. "We have just installed an electric lift to the top floor where your rooms are. It has been designed by the same company that installed the ones in the Eiffel Tower. We have had some minor mechanical problems with it, but I'm sure you will find it very useful, as you shall see."

The "lift" turns out to be a shaky metal cage in a vertical shaft, pulled up by a single cable. Only two of you can crowd in at a time. One trip is made with just you and your textbooks, as you go up to your room on the fourth floor.

"Of course I don't expect you to spend all of your time studying," Miss Seymour says, as she helps you to unpack. "But I do expect a certain amount of diligence."

When you are finished unpacking, you and Miss Seymour go back to the first floor, where everyone is now waiting for the trip to the Louvre.

"Since we've been cooped up in a train for

many hours, I thought it would do us all good to walk there," your father says. "It's not that far."

After a few blocks, you reach the river and start over one of the many bridges that Miss Seymour has told you about.

"This is called the Pont des Arts, the Bridge of the Arts," Miss Seymour says. "Very appropriate, don't you think?"

Halfway across, Miss Seymour points out the Île de la Cité not far upstream. The twin towers of Notre-Dame, you notice, rise high above the other buildings on the island.

On the other side of the river, a long line of ornate palaces surrounded by acres of gardens stretches along the bank.

"These were once the palaces of the kings of France," your father says. "The king at the time of the French Revolution, Louis XVI, and his queen, Marie Antoinette, lost their heads—literally—on the guillotine here. His palace was then established as the Musée Central des Arts—the Central Museum of Arts—by the revolutionary government. In it they placed the large number of artworks all the kings had collected. To this they added the private collections of the aristocrats who had fled the country."

→ → → → → → → → → → → → →

Go on to the next page.

"If we walk around to the side entrance," Miss Seymour says, "I think we can avoid the crowds."

You and your parents follow her across a wide park and around to the side of one of the large buildings.

Inside, you go up a wide staircase, down several wide hallways, and through many large galleries filled with oversized classical landscapes.

"There are so many masterpieces here, through miles and miles of galleries," Miss Seymour says. "I thought I would show Indy just a few of my favorites to start with. Up ahead is one. It's by an artist named Géricault, and it's titled *The Raft of the* Medusa."

You look over at the large painting. It shows a raft full of men being tossed about in a violently stormy sea.

"This shows the seamen from the ill-fated ship *Medusa* just at the point where a rescue ship there in the distance has sighted them," Miss Seymour says.

"It's certainly dramatic," you say. "It's almost as if the artist were there seeing the scene."

"It is a remarkable painting," your father says. "Someday I suspect that photography will take the place of paintings like this in recording historical events."

"You mean with those funny boxes the photographers set up on tripods?" your mother asks. "Why it takes them ever so long to take a picture."

"Professor Jones is probably right," Miss Seymour says. "Who knows? Maybe someday cameras will be small enough to carry around in your hand. There are certainly marvelous advances in science going on today. Who would have thought just a few years ago that we could *fly*?"

Miss Seymour guides you and your parents through several more galleries. There are hundreds of paintings, all of which you have to admit are great. You particularly like the *Lace Maker* by an artist named Vermeer, and *La Bohémiénne* by Frans Hals. They are both so full of light.

"And now for what some people consider the most important painting in the Louvre," Miss Seymour says, as you move forward.

"Which one is that?" you ask.

"You'll see," Miss Seymour says, as she leads you to a painting in the corner of yet another gallery. It is dimly lit from the skylight high above.

Miss Seymour and your parents stand there for a moment, all entranced by the picture.

"No matter how many times I see the *Mona Lisa*," your father says, "I always see it anew."

"It took Leonardo da Vinci four years to paint it," Miss Seymour says. "Think of it. The woman whose portrait this is had to hold that faint smile for many hours almost every day for four years. It is said that Leonardo had musicians playing in his studio whenever he was painting her, as well as singers and comedians to keep her amused."

You sit on a gallery couch back from the painting and start to doze off while Miss Seymour is lecturing.

"Do you think you could smile like that? I mean like this," Miss Seymour calls over to you, trying to imitate the slight smile on the portrait. "Or do you not like this painting as much as some of the others?"

→ → → → → → → → → → → → →

Her question shakes you back to consciousness. "I do like the painting," you say with some conviction.

"Maybe you'll like some of the modern artists better," Miss Seymour says. "Tomorrow we'll go to the Luxembourg Galleries and see some of their paintings."

An hour later, you are all back at the hotel. Then you are out again for dinner at a small candlelit restaurant around the corner.

"Your mother and I have to pack tonight. We're leaving for the south of France early tomorrow morning. Miss Seymour is going to stay here in Paris to finish her correspondence," your father says.

"You'll have to decide if you want to go with us or stay here with Miss Seymour until we get back," your mother says.

"We're going to have a quiet holiday in the wine country," your father says. "I'm not sure how exciting it will be, but you'll be able to read and go hiking in the countryside."

"You'll have plenty of free time here—as long as you get your lessons done," Miss Seymour says.

You'd certainly like to get out from under Miss Seymour's thumb. On the other hand, you'd like to see more of Paris and all the things you've read about.

You look at your parents, then at Miss Seymour, as you try to decide what you are going to do.

→ → → → → → → → → → → → →

If you decide to stay in Paris with Miss Seymour, turn to page 39.

If you decide to go with your parents, turn to page 98.

You decide to go to Picasso's studio.

You leave the café, and the narrow, twisting street behind it turns into a stairway that goes up and up. Off to your right is a huge white edifice with onion-shaped domes. "That's the Cathedral of Sacré-Coeur," Norman says.

Finally you reach the top. You, Norman, Fernande, and Braque are out of breath. Picasso, however, seems ready to run back down and start all over again.

You come to the back of a multistoried, ramshackle wooden building clinging to the side of the hill. The roof is covered with skylights, and stovepipes stick out of it haphazardly. All the windows look very dirty. You walk around to the front, where the top story faces the street.

"Here we are," Picasso says. "Thirteen Rue Ravignan."

The five of you go in through an unlocked door and down a rickety stairway to Picasso's studio below.

→ → → → → → → → → → → →

Go on to the next page.

16

There is hardly any furniture inside—a few benches and a mattress in the corner—and what is there is thoroughly paint splattered. A large white cat crouches at the end of a long shelf otherwise filled with African sculpture. Paintings are stacked several deep against the walls. There is an easel in the center of the large room. Next to it a taboret is piled with tubes of paint, brushes, and sticks of pastel.

You and Norman sit down on one of the benches, while Braque and Fernande engage in conversation.

→ → → → → → → → → → → →

Turn to page 42.

You turn and pet the monkey a few times as the accordionist lurches into a brisk march tune. Then Miss Seymour guides you down the street with one hand while holding an open guidebook in the other.

Across the street is a pastry shop, its window filled with cakes. A delicious scent from inside drifts across the street. You suddenly realize how hungry you are. You tug on Miss Seymour's sleeve and point to the store.

"Can I . . . ?" you ask.

"Certainly not," Miss Seymour says. "You've only just had breakfast, and I want to get to the Luxembourg Museum before it opens. I see in the guidebook that they're having a special show of paintings by Degas, a painter whose work I love."

Miss Seymour walks along briskly, with you hurrying behind. "We could take a taxi, but it'll be almost as fast on foot, and we'll save some money," she says.

After a number of blocks, you turn a corner and see a large park with flower gardens and many statues and walkways. You walk past a large pool surrounded by trees and an ornate fountain.

→ → → → → → → → → → → → → →

Go on to the next page.

"It says here in the guidebook," Miss Seymour says, as she hurries you along toward a large, domed building, "that there are fifty-eight acres of gardens surrounding the palace complex. It was built by one of the French queens, Marie de Médicis, to remind her of a palace in her hometown of Florence, Italy."

The buildings sure are huge, you think. But you wouldn't want to live in one.

Inside the gallery, you and Miss Seymour look at the paintings by Degas.

"This one is called *The Absinthe Drinker,* and the one over here, that's *The Laundress.* What do you think of them?" Miss Seymour asks.

"They're certainly different from the ones in the Louvre. The people in them are sort of . . . fuzzy," you say.

"It's a new style called impressionism," she says. "It tries to depict what the eye sees at a glance. The artist paints what he *sees* directly rather than what he knows about it. Do you understand?"

"Not . . . exactly," you say. "But I'm trying."

"It's a fresh, natural way for the artist to see nature. The impressionists are trying to show how patterns of light and color are recorded directly by our senses."

→ → → → → → → → → → → →

Go on to the next page.

A boy about fourteen years old is sitting nearby, sketching one of the paintings. He listens to Miss Seymour's speech, then looks up from his sketchbook. "I like the way you explained impressionism," he says. "That's just the way *I* feel about it."

Miss Seymour looks over at his drawing. "You are very talented," she says.

"I've been drawing for a long time—ever since I can remember," the boy says. "I think I was born wanting to be an artist. My name is Norman—Norman Rockwell."

"You're American?" you ask.

"From New York City."

"I'm from Princeton, New Jersey," you say. "That makes us practically neighbors."

"So you're going to be an impressionist painter," Miss Seymour says.

Norman laughs. "Impressionist? Perhaps. I try to learn something from all the artists. Yesterday I was sketching over in the Louvre."

"We were over there yesterday, too. Somehow we missed you," you say.

"I'm not surprised," Norman says. "I'm told that there are eight miles of galleries in the Louvre. I've spent weeks roaming through them, and I haven't seen all of them by a long shot."

"Which painter do you like best?" you ask.

"I like them all. Come, I'll show the two of you the works of some more," he says.

Norman leads you and Miss Seymour out of the Degas exhibit to another gallery filled with different impressionist painters. "Look at this one," he says. "It's by a painter named Seurat. Look at it up close and then far away."

You go up and look at the canvas from a few inches away. "All I see are little dots of different bright colors," you say.

"Now look at it from a distance," Norman says.

You walk across to the other side of the gallery, then look back at the painting. "Now I see a landscape filled with trees and people," you say. "Amazing."

"Seurat paints only with little dots of pure color. He lets your eye mix them to form images and other colors. It's very scientific."

Norman takes you and Miss Seymour around to the paintings of different impressionist artists—Manet, Pissarro, and Renoir. "You see," he says, "they all have different techniques for giving a direct impression to the eye."

You have a feeling that Miss Seymour already knows a lot of this, but she is very impressed with Norman and is letting him tell you about the paintings in his own words.

"Whew!" you say. "I never imagined all of these things could be going on."

"You haven't seen anything yet," Norman says. "Wait until I show you the work of the fauvists."

→ → → → → → → → → → → → →

Go on to the next page.

"I think this is enough for one day," Miss Seymour interrupts. "Tell your teacher where you're going, Norman, and I'll treat you and Indy to lunch somewhere nearby."

"My teacher and his family are out of town visiting Versailles for a couple of days," Norman says.

"You mean you're wandering around Paris all by yourself!" Miss Seymour exclaims.

"Not exactly . . . but something like that," he says.

You're beginning to like your new friend more and more.

Miss Seymour leads you and Norman, his sketchbook under his arm, back to the Boulevard St. Germain. There you enter a small café across the busy square from the stately old church of St-Germain-des-Prés.

"Am I ever hungry," you tell Norman, as the three of you sit down at a table. "Do you know what we had for breakfast? It was—"

"I know," Norman interrupts. "You can't get a decent New York breakfast in all of Paris. It's the only thing I don't like about this place."

After you order your food, Norman immediately sets to sketching the other customers seated at some of the nearby tables. You look over his shoulder. The drawings are very realistic, not at all what you thought they'd be.

→ → → → → → → → → → → →

Go on to the next page.

"Where did you learn to draw like that?" you ask.

"Everyone asks me that. It's just a gift . . . I guess," Norman says.

You were talking about the fauvists back at the museum," Miss Seymour says. "I'll have to confess that I don't know much about them, though I've heard the name."

"The fauvists had an exhibition a few years ago which really shook up the art world—even more than the impressionists did," Norman says. "Some of the artists' names are Matisse, Derain, Dufy, and Vlaminck. One critic who saw the show thought the paintings reminded him of a collection of wild animals. The nickname 'Fauves' or 'wild beasts' caught on. Even the painters involved loved the name and adopted it for themselves. They use pure, bright colors in bold, flat patterns. Also, they use colors the way they *feel* about things, not the way they actually are. By that, I mean a tree trunk might be purple. The sky could be green, and the trees yellow."

"Sounds a bit out of control to me," Miss Seymour says, as your dishes of food arrive. "I think I prefer the old masters."

"I wouldn't worry too much about the fauvists," Norman says. "I think they've already had their day—styles come and go. But they did have a lot of influence. Painters like Picasso learned a lot from them."

"Picasso?" Miss Seymour says. "I've heard that name before, but I'm not familiar with his work."

"You should see the things *he's* doing," Norman says. "He's combining all these influences— impressionism, fauvism, and even primitive and African art."

"African art?" Miss Seymour asks. "I'd like to see that."

"I can show you if—" Norman starts.

"Maybe later," Miss Seymour interrupts, looking at her watch. I have to go to the post office. You two finish your lunch and talk. I'll be back soon, so *don't* leave."

Miss Seymour then runs off down the avenue.

"What do you think of Miss Seymour?" you ask Norman.

"Oh, she seems all right, though I'm glad she's not *my* tutor."

"Your tutor is out of town, you said?"

"He told the concierge of my hotel to keep an eye on me," Norman explains. "But I found a way of sneaking in and out. I'm only on the second floor—so I have no trouble climbing down. There's an alley behind the hotel that leads to a side street."

"Are you ever lucky," you say. "I'm on the fourth floor. I don't know if I could get down."

"You could give it a try tonight—but don't kill yourself, if you know what I mean. Be careful."

→ → → → → → → → → → → →

Go on to the next page.

26

"I'll find some way of—" you start.

"Say, I know of a café where all the artists hang out," Norman says. "It's called Le Lapin Agile. Why don't we go over there right now? This painter I was talking about, Picasso, might be there. He's quite a guy."

"I have to wait here until Miss Seymour comes back," you say.

"She's probably going to be a long time. The post office is a number of blocks away. Anyway, we can leave a note telling her where we are in case she gets back first."

"I don't know . . ." you say.

"Come on, we're in Paris. Let's have some fun. You've got to take risks."

You know that Miss Seymour will really be upset if she gets back and you're not here. Perhaps you could ask her for permission to go when she returns. If you wait, she might want to see the café Norman is talking about herself.

On the other hand, she is just as liable to take you back to the hotel and start you in on your books. This may be your only chance to see the artists' café.

→ → → → → → → → → → → →

*If you decide to wait for Miss Seymour,
turn to page 90.*

*If you decide to go to the café with Norman,
turn to page 55.*

You decide to escape across the rooftops. You put on your jacket and quietly leave your room, closing the door behind you very carefully. Silently you tiptoe to the communal bathroom at the end of the hall, stand on the edge of the tub, and gently raise the small window over it. Then, pushing off with your feet, you pull yourself through it.

Fortunately, the roof outside is a drop of only a few feet. It covers a back section of the hotel. You close the window behind you and edge along the roof in the dark.

Not far away, there is an open window, dimly lit on the inside. You see a heavyset man taking off his eyeglasses and advancing toward it. You stiffen against the side of the building as the man reaches outside to close the shutters.

You take a deep breath and ease past the now-closed window. You come to the end of the roof and look down at the night hawks hurrying along the street far below. You shiver for a moment, but not from the cold. You're nervous, but you pull yourself together and look for a way down to the next level.

→ → → → → → → → → → → → →

Turn to page 57.

"We'll take the metro, the underground railway," Norman says. "I've got some change."

"I thought you said we wouldn't be away long," you say.

"I never said that," Norman says.

"I should go back," you say.

"The metro is very fast," Norman says. "It travels many blocks in just seconds. It's the latest thing. We have one in New York City. They're run by electricity."

"Well, if you're sure," you say. "I haven't ridden on one yet."

"All the more reason to try it. Look, there's a metro entrance over there."

"That's a metro entrance?" you say, looking at a small structure made up of intertwining, fantastic forms.

"It's what they call art nouveau," Norman says. "It uses forms out of nature, like tree trunks and twisting vines. The metro started a whole new style of its own—*le style métro*."

Inside the building, you pay an attendant and go down a long flight of steps to a tunnel below. A double set of tracks runs between two wide platforms. The tracks disappear into a dark tunnel in both directions.

"We're on the right platform to get the train we need," Norman says. "Our stop is the Opéra on Boulevard Haussmann."

→ → → → → → → → → → → →

Turn to page 31.

30207

Soon you see two points of light way down the tunnel. They gradually grow into the headlights of the underground train. The train rumbles into the station and comes to a stop. An attendant opens the car door from the inside, and you and Norman step in. You both sit down on one of the wide wicker seats inside.

The train is crowded with workers going to or from their jobs. Some are carrying baskets filled with long loaves of French bread called baguettes. The aroma fills the car.

"That sure smells good," you say.

"Makes me hungry all over again," Norman says. "We can get something to eat at Le Lapin Agile."

After several stops, Norman motions for you to follow him off. You come out of the metro station on an island in the middle of the street. The Opéra building itself looms in front of you like a giant wedding cake.

"See, that didn't take long," Norman says.

"You're right," you say. "It was a great ride."

Norman leads you away from the metro station and down several side streets. You come out into a small square bustling with activity. Le Lapin Agile is on the other side of the square with its chairs and tables crowding the sidewalk in front. You can hear an accordionist playing somewhere inside.

→ → → → → → → → → → → → →

Go on to the next page.

You and Norman go over and sit at a table on the sidewalk. Your attention is drawn to two men sitting at a nearby table examining several large drawings. One of them has shoulder-length white hair and a beard to match. He is dressed in a dark suit with waistcoat and a bow tie. The other one appears to be in his twenties. He is bullnecked, with fierce, dark eyes beneath a mop of black hair. He is wearing a woolen jersey and baggy pants.

"The older man is Degas," Norman whispers to you. "The other one is the painter I was telling you about, Pablo Picasso."

"*The* Degas?" you say. "The one who did the paintings we saw today?"

"That's right," Norman says.

As you watch, a waitress sets a glass of red wine on the table where Degas and Picasso are sitting. At the same moment, Degas, in the process of explaining a fine point about one of Picasso's drawings, makes a sweeping gesture with his hand, tipping over the wine.

"Olé!" Picasso shouts, as he quickly smears the spilled wine over part of the drawing. "There," he says. "I thank you. I think that improves it a lot."

→ → → → → → → → → → → → →

Go on to the next page.

Degas, apparently somewhat nearsighted, bends over to examine the drawing. "Monsieur Picasso," he says, "I'm afraid nothing could improve your drawing. It is hopelessly bad." He looks as if he is about to tear it up.

A large, very attractive woman with great almond eyes sitting next to Picasso reaches over and snatches the drawing out of harm's way.

"I must warn you," Degas tells Picasso, "what you are doing to art is destructive. You are throwing out perspective and composition."

"Because we need a new way of seeing," Picasso says.

"I look, I see. But you look and do not see," Degas says, exasperated.

"I see the *real* shape, the real form," Picasso says.

"You play with words, Picasso, that is your art" Degas says. "But your friends are laughing behind your back—or worse."

"Who?" Picasso asks.

"Matisse for one. And that Russian collector Shchukin. He actually wept telling me what a loss to French art you are. With all your talent..."

"You may be right about Shchukin," Picasso says. "I mean, what does he know about art, after all? But you're wrong about Matisse. I know he respects my work. I think he is even a little jealous of it. As for how *you* draw, why I can do that in my sleep."

The accordionist, still playing comes out from inside the café and squeezes a finale right behind Picasso and Degas. "Enough, my friends," he says. "Picasso, leave the old man alone. He has already carved his niche in the history of art."

"Thank you, Monsieur Braque," Degas says to the accordion player, "but I am quite capable of standing up for myself."

"Monsieur Degas," the woman next to Picasso says, "Pablo doesn't mean to offend you, he just—"

"I certainly do mean to offend him!" Picasso shouts indignantly.

Degas pushes away from the table and stands up, smoothing down his waistcoat and trying to maintain his dignity. Then he walks off in a huff.

"I don't think you should talk to Monsieur Degas that way," Norman pipes up. "He is a great painter."

"You're wrong," Picasso says, turning toward your table. "I can say whatever I like."

"I think we'd better get back to the metro," you whisper to Norman.

Picasso gets up from his table and takes a revolver from his belt. He comes over to your table and glares at Norman.

→ → → → → → → → → → → →

Go on to the next page.

36

"You insulted me!" Picasso says in mock anger.

"You don't scare me," Norman says.

Braque, who has somehow put on boxing gloves while this is going on, steps in between. "If you shoot him, I'll punch you back to Spain where you belong," he tells Picasso.

"Georges, you stay out of this," Picasso says as he grabs Norman by the collar. "Okay this time," he adds. "But if you're insinuating that I can't paint like Degas, you need an art lesson. I'm taking you to my studio to prove it to you. This is war!"

Everybody laughs. You give a sigh of relief— for a moment you thought they might really be fighting.

Picasso introduces you to Georges Braque, the accordionist, but also an artist, and the young woman, Fernande. "Now we must climb the Butte to my studio in the Bateau-Lavoir!" Picasso exclaims.

"I should be getting back to the café where my tutor is. She must be waiting for me by this time," you say.

"And miss the chance to see Picasso's studio?" Norman says.

→ → → → → → → → → → → → →

Turn to page 38.

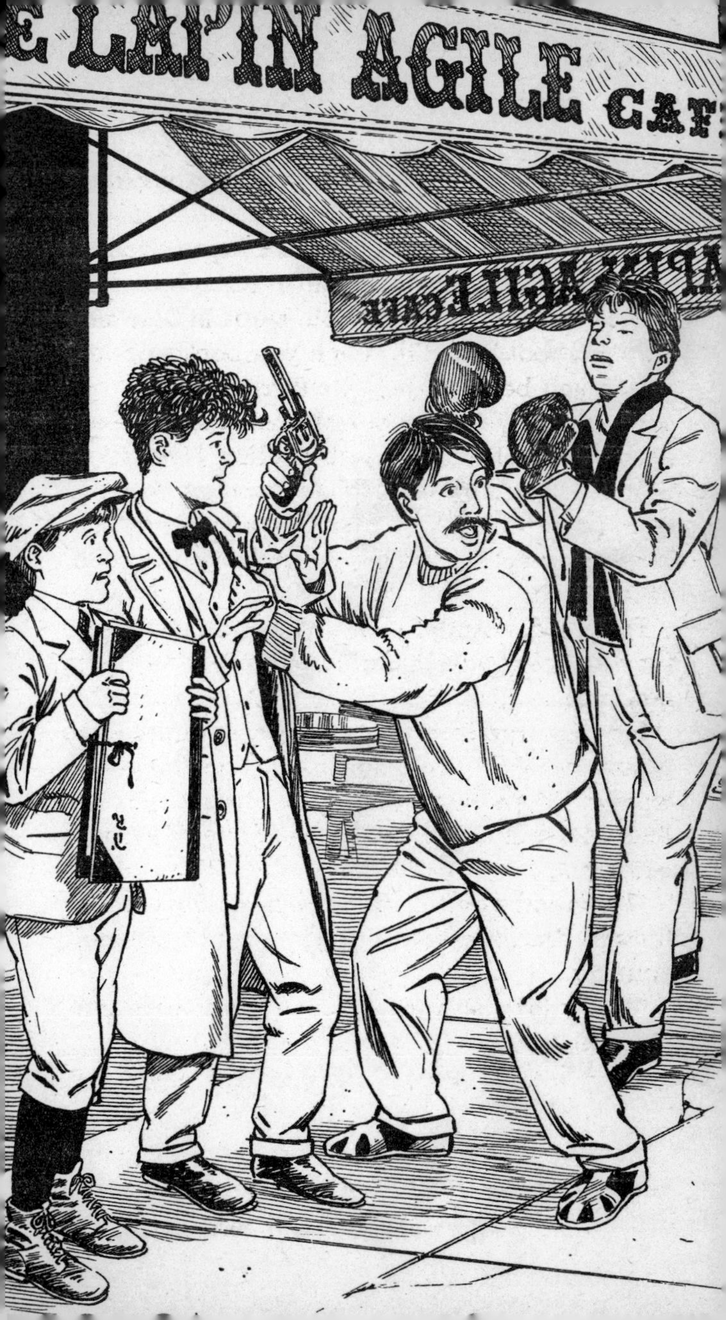
LAPIN AGILE

Picasso and Braque look at you expectantly.
Norman is right in a way, this is a chance you
shouldn't pass up. But you can visit Picasso's
studio later, maybe even with Miss Seymour. If
you don't get back now, you may not be visiting
anything.

← ← ← ← ← ← ← ← ← ← ← ←

*If you decide to go to Picasso's studio now,
turn to page 15.*

→ → → → → → → → → → → →

*If you decide to go back to the café where Miss
Seymour is waiting, turn to page 95.*

You decide to stay in Paris with Miss Seymour. Early the next morning, you have a continental breakfast at the hotel, which to your disgust you find is just a small croissant and a cup of light coffee called café au lait. After that, you and Miss Seymour help your parents load the taxi that will take them back to the railroad station. You look at Miss Seymour and then at your parents, wondering if you made the right choice. It's not that you don't like Miss Seymour. You secretly admire her in many ways. It's just that sometimes she can be a little unreasonable.

You are about to change your mind and ask your parents if you can go with them when Miss Seymour distracts your attention by steering you over to a barrel accordionist with a pet monkey begging for money.

"He won't bite," the accordionist says.

→ → → → → → → → → → → →

Go on to the next page.

Miss Seymour takes a coin from her purse and drops it into the small metal cup the monkey is carrying. The coin clinks dully on the bottom.

You turn back just in time to see your parents waving good-bye from the taxi as it moves away down the street.

You sigh inwardly. There's no turning back now. Like it or not, you're stuck with Miss Seymour until they come back.

← ← ← ← ← ← ← ← ← ← ← ←

Turn to page 17.

Picasso tacks a large sheet of heavy paper on his easel and immediately starts in on a composition in pastels. It's a variation of *The Absinthe Drinker* you saw in the Luxembourg Museum. You recognize it immediately.

You and Norman watch as Picasso works furiously. "Do you like my Degas?" he asks, as he finishes.

"It's terrific!" you say.

"So you see, I can do what Degas does, but Degas *can't* do what I do. Come, I'll show you."

Picasso leads you to the back of his studio. A large painting, approximately eight feet square, is leaning against the wall. "I call this *Les Demoiselles d'Avignon*, in honor of five ladies I knew in a section of Barcelona," he says. "You see the faces of the two women on the right, they are like the ones on the pieces of African sculpture over there."

The faces of the women in the painting are flat, with twisted noses. They *are* sort of like the African sculptures, you realize. But somehow Picasso's faces look much more fierce.

"What do you think?" Picasso asks.

"It's different, all right," you say.

"I think it's great," Norman says. "Would you mind if I sketched it?"

"Go right ahead. I'll be back to take a look," Picasso says as he goes to the front of the studio.

Braque comes over while Norman is sketching. "Picasso is making us look at everything in a new way," he says. "Look at this." He pulls a small painting out from behind the *Demoiselles*.

"This is a landscape," Braque says. "See how it's made up of cubes? That's why they call us cubists."

Norman is just finishing his sketch when Picasso comes back. "Let me see," Picasso says, taking the sketch from Norman. He studies it for a second, then whips out a pencil and signs it "Picasso."

"Now it's a genuine Picasso," he says.

"Even though I drew it?" Norman says.

"But *I* signed it," Picasso says.

"I don't know—" Norman starts.

"It's all a matter of how you look at it," Picasso interrupts. "Here, look!"

→ → → → → → → → → → → →
Go on to the next page.

Picasso grabs a pair of bicycle handlebars from behind one of the paintings. He puts the handlebars inside out and upside down behind his head, then crouches. "What am I?" he asks.

"A bull?" you say.

"Right, a bull—or maybe a sculpture of a bull, or the idea of a bull. And what are these?" he asks, standing up again and handing you the handlebars.

"Bicycle handlebars," you say.

"And who am I?"

"Pablo Picasso," Norman says.

"You see? One minute a handlebar, the next a bull, then Picasso. Things change like magic—in our minds. And that is what art should be about. Do you understand?"

"I... think so," you say, still somewhat puzzled.

"And now I'm going back to Le Lapin Agile. All this talk has given me an appetite."

Picasso sprints outside with the rest of you following. It's clear that he wants to race everyone down.

He disappears down the hill with Fernande, the two of them giggling like children.

"Don't try to go too fast," Braque warns you. "You can kill yourself on these stairs."

"Miss Seymour is going to kill me for sure when I get back," you say.

→ → → → → → → → → → → → →

Go on to the next page.

"Too late to worry about that now," Norman says.

Norman's right. And so is Braque. You follow his advice and take your time going down the stairs. This gives you a chance to look around. Just behind you, the massive structure of the Sacré-Coeur is a brilliant white in the late-afternoon sun. Ahead of you is a panoramic view of Paris—a sea of slate roofs and chimney pots stretching into the distance. Far below, the bright ribbon of the Seine divides the city in two. Way off to the right, the Eiffel Tower rises up into the sky, and in the distance to the left are the twin towers of Notre-Dame Cathedral.

You keep going down until you reach the narrow streets below. Soon you see Le Lapin Agile up ahead.

You see Picasso and Fernande out in front arguing with somebody momentarily hidden on the other side of them. Your heart sinks when you realize that it's Miss Seymour.

"But this has been the greatest education for your student—learning the true meaning of art," Fernande says.

"I'll be the one to decide that," Miss Seymour says.

She suddenly sees you coming and stands there, hands on her hips, glaring in your direction. Even Picasso backs off a bit when he sees the expression on her face.

"If you want to make a run for it, you can hide out at my place," Norman whispers in your ear.

"No, I'd better just face it," you say nervously.

"*You* are going right back to the hotel and not getting out of my sight until your parents come back," Miss Seymour tells you angrily.

"And as for you," she says to Norman, shaking her finger at him, "you may have a lot of talent for someone your age, but you are a trouble-maker, and whoever is supposed to be looking after you is not doing their job."

→ → → → → → → → → → →

Go on to the next page.

While this is going on, Norman has torn out a slip of paper from the back of his sketchbook and is writing something down. He crumbles it into a ball and slips it into your pocket when Miss Seymour turns to scold Picasso.

"Perfect!" Picasso exclaims, holding up his fingers to square off a picture of Miss Seymour.

"What is?" she says angrily.

"That look. I must paint it. Would you sit for a portrait?"

"Humph!" Miss Seymour says. "You are being insulting."

"Not at all. I am an artist. I am Picasso. Haven't you heard of me?"

"Not really," Miss Seymour says. "Only a few things. Well, at any rate, I'm not holding you responsible. I'm sure your intentions were good—helping my student learn about art."

"Absolutely," Picasso says, bowing.

→ → → → → → → → → → → → →

Go on to the next page.

50

You wave good-bye to Norman and your other friends as Miss Seymour drags you off down the street toward the metro. You can hardly wait to read the note that Norman slipped into your pocket.

"You'll stay in your room and work on your French grammar before you turn in," Miss Seymour says back at the hotel.

Your small desk by the window of your room is piled high with books. They are lit by a double oil lamp.

"See that you are in bed by nine o'clock. *Bonsoir*—good-night," she says as she closes the door of your room going out.

You sit at the foot of your bed for a while, feeling bad. After a while you go over to the door and open it a crack. Everything is quiet in the hallway outside. Miss Seymour's door is slightly ajar, and a yellow shaft of light cuts across the floor of the hallway. Soon the light blinks out. You guess that Miss Seymour is turning in for the night.

Remembering the note that Norman stuffed in your pocket, you take it out and smooth it flat. It reads:

If you can sneak out tonight, meet me at the Moulin-Rouge. Picasso will be there too. Take the metro to Place Pigalle.

No way, you say to yourself at first. That's all I need—to get caught by Miss Seymour trying to sneak out. On the other hand, you reason, if I *do* go out and get back before she wakes up, she'll never find out.

You look out the window. There's a sheer drop four stories to the street. Then another idea hits you.

You go out of your room and tiptoe down to the small communal bathroom at the end of the hall. Inside, you stand on the edge of the bathtub and look out the small window above it.

Outside is a series of rooftops starting just below the window. As your eyes get used to the dim light, you notice that there is a series of progressively smaller buildings, like a giant stairway. If you could get across them, you might be able to find a way down to the street.

You climb down from the tub and go back to your room. Sitting at your desk, you gaze out your window at the lights of Paris, wondering what to do. You think of Miss Seymour. Then you think of Norman, probably living it up with the artists in the Parisian night spots. You can't just stay in your room, you decide. You've got to sneak out and find Norman. But how? you wonder.

You could try to get across the rooftops, but that might be dangerous. Besides, you don't like heights.

→ → → → → → → → → → → →

Go on to the next page.

54

Maybe you could sneak past Miss Seymour's room and past the concierge at the front door, you think. But the dangers of climbing over the rooftops are nothing compared to what would happen to you if Miss Seymour caught you sneaking out of the front door of the hotel. Still, it might be worth a try.

You sit at your desk thinking about the comparative risks involved.

← ← ← ← ← ← ← ← ← ← ← ←
If you decide to go across the rooftops, turn to page 27.

→ → → → → → → → → → → →
If you decide to try to sneak out the front door of the hotel, turn to page 86.

You decide to go with Norman to the café. You tear off a piece of paper from the back of the small diary that you always carry with you and write a note to Miss Seymour.

Dear Miss Seymour,
Norman and I are going to a café called
Le Lapin Agile to see if we can find the artist
named Picasso. We will be back soon.

Indy

You call the waiter over and give him the note. "Miss Seymour is my tutor," you tell him. "She will be back to pay our bill if we don't get back first."

Then you and Norman hurry away from the café while the waiter looks at the note and scratches his head.

"He thinks we're skipping out on the bill," you say.

"You're right. He'll probably call the police. But at least he isn't running after us."

You think about going back, but you are already a couple of blocks away from the café. You might as well keep going, you convince yourself.

← ← ← ← ← ← ← ← ← ← ← ← ←

Turn to page 28.

You find a drainpipe that leads from the gutters at your feet to the next story below. You reach down and shake the pipe. It seems solid enough. You're used to climbing trees back home, and shimmying down a drainpipe is not that much different.

You carefully climb down to the roof below. Now you have only two stories to go. Unfortunately, the drainpipe ends right there.

Nearby, the high, sharply pitched roof of a smaller building next door is only a couple of feet away. You jump over and slide down the slates, coming to a stop at the gutter along the bottom of the roof.

Just below you is a line of clothes washing—bloomers, nightdresses, and sheets. Below the laundry is a large doghouse.

You jump off into midair, grabbing the sheets on the line and swinging in an arc as they come loose. This breaks your fall a bit, but you still land heavily on the roof of the doghouse. You look around, then jump off the side and down to the ground.

At the same moment, something large and dark comes charging out of the doghouse, its teeth clashing after you and growling in anger.

→ → → → → → → → → → → →

Go on to the next page.

You dash for the exit gate of the courtyard as the dog streaks toward you. Suddenly, just before it catches up with you, the animal is brought to a violent halt. The links of its restraining chain tighten with the strain but hold fast.

Out of breath, you stop and look back into the darkness for a moment. The dog looks more like a leopard, its yellow eyes glowing in the darkness. He continues to bark at you wildly, but you're out of danger.

You go out to the street and head toward the metro station a few blocks away. Fortunately, your parents gave you some change before they left. You pay the attendant your fare and get on the next train.

Sitting inside, you are surprised to see half a dozen people all dressed in brightly colored tights and leotards. One of them wears a blue and yellow checkered shirt and pants with one red leg and one green leg. Another is quietly juggling several balls and humming to himself. Their costumes look just a bit tattered.

You walk over to one of them. "Is this train going to Place Pigalle?" you ask.

"Ah, Place Pigalle, but of course! That is where we are headed. Are you going to the outdoor circus to see us?"

"I didn't know there was one," you say.

"Well now you do. Take it from me, François, our show is very good. Acrobats, jugglers, death-defying feats. Pepé," he says to another member of the group seated next to him, "show our friend."

Pepé drops a large ball he has been holding in his lap to the floor of the train. He quickly jumps onto the ball, rolling it under him back and forth without losing his balance. He rolls up to the end of the car and then back again before sitting down with the ball in his lap.

"That's very good," you say. "But Pepé doesn't smile. Does he enjoy doing that?"

"The life of an acrobat is very hard, particularly when *you* do not come to see him," François says.

"I'd like to," you say. "But I have to meet my friends, Norman and Picasso."

"Pablo Picasso, the artist?" François asks.

"That's the one," you say.

"Monsieur Picasso is a great fan of ours. He is always at the circus, watching us and sketching. He sketched my portrait and gave it to me," François says. He turns to a boy about your age who is dressed as a harlequin. "Where did I put that sketch by Picasso?"

"It's in your bag, Papa," the boy says, handing François a small, battered valise.

"I think this is it," François says, pulling a small sketch out of the valise. "No, this one is of you, my son, leading a horse."

→ → → → → → → → → → → → →

Go on to the next page.

You look at the sketch. It's unmistakably the boy, and it's signed "Picasso."

"Well, I'll find it one of these days," François says. "Or maybe Picasso will do another one for me. But come to think of it, I haven't seen him for a while. I hear that he is becoming famous. Perhaps he is too busy for the circus now."

"I'll ask him about it," you say. "I hope to see him later at the Moulin-Rouge."

"What a coincidence!" François exclaims. "We are going to perform in the square in front of the Moulin-Rouge tonight."

"You don't have a circus tent or anything?" you ask.

"Goodness no, we are the *cirque forain,* travelers and wanderers. We perform anywhere, anytime. In cabarets and in the street."

"At the zoo, Papa," the boy says. "And at the racetrack."

"Everywhere!" François exclaims, jumping up on the seat and spreading his arms. "Even in the metro."

Immediately, Pepé jumps up and starts riding once again on his ball. François starts juggling six small balls of different colors. His son starts walking on his hands. The rest of the performers do cartwheels up and down the aisle.

→ → → → → → → → → → → → →

Go on to the next page.

The other passengers in the car applaud, and some throw small coins at the performers. The performers pick up the coins from the floor without losing a beat in their acts.

"And here we are at Place Pigalle," François announces, as the train comes to a stop in the station.

Outside the metro station, you follow the performers up a long street sloping upward. They march along as if in some grand parade.

Soon, up ahead, across a square packed with people, you see a red windmill rising above the large entrance to the Moulin-Rouge cabaret.

Your new friends manage to find an open space in the center of the square and go into their acts. You wave good-bye to them as you head for the entrance to the cabaret.

Pressing though the crowd, you go in. You stand there openmouthed for a moment at the sight. The place is packed, both on the dance floor and at the tables. A band is beating out a deafening rhythm.

The whole place is lit with Venetian glass globes. Multicolored streamers hang from the ceiling, in the center of which is a large rotating ball completely covered with small mirrors. It showers moving splinters of light on the crowd below.

You spot Picasso. You can't miss him—he is sitting close to the band. Next to him are Norman, Braque, and Fernande.

You work your way through the crowd and over to their table.

"You made it!" Norman exclaims, jumping up.

"Good to see you again," Braque says, shaking your hand.

"It wasn't easy getting out of the hotel," you say. "But I made it. I even ran into a crowd of circus performers on the way over."

"Circus performers?" Picasso asks.

"Yes, they're in the square outside," you say. "One of them named François said that you painted his portrait."

"François is here? I'll be back," Picasso says, heading for the door.

→ → → → → → → → → → → →

Go on to the next page.

"I'm glad you were able to come," Fernande tells you. "I wanted to invite you to a big party we're having for Henri Rousseau. He's Picasso's favorite painter. Pablo feels that *he* discovered him. He was walking by a junk shop when he saw one of Rousseau's paintings leaning against a wall inside. It was a jungle scene done in a primitive manner. The man running the shop wanted to sell it to Picasso for only a few pennies, telling him it would be cheaper than buying a new canvas to paint on. Pablo brought it home and added it to his collection. Since then, Picasso has been trying to get people to appreciate Rousseau's art. Pablo has also invited Degas to the party. He is going to trick him into signing the 'Degas' that you saw Picasso draw earlier in his studio."

"Isn't that kind of a dirty trick?" you say.

"Not really. He wants to prove that no one, not even Degas himself, can tell a Degas painted by Picasso from a real Degas," Fernande says.

Picasso comes back to the table with François and the performers. He seats them at the table next to his, then signals to one of the waiters.

"Give my friends anything they want," Picasso says. Then he calls the waiter in closer and whispers, "Did you finish *it*?"

"But of course," the waiter says. "I have it in the back. Don't forget, you now owe me a painting."

"Bring it out, then," Picasso says.

"Here?" the waiter asks.

"Why not?" Picasso says. "I want to show it to my friends."

The waiter disappears for a few minutes and then returns with a box. Picasso takes the box and hands it to you as the waiter nods and walks away.

"Open the box and you'll understand about cubism," Picasso tells you, looking at Braque with a smile.

You open the box. Inside is a small model of a biplane, powered with a windup rubber band.

"Now you know why Picasso sometimes calls me Wilbur Wright," Braque says, leaning over your shoulder. "We are the pioneers of the flight of imagination."

"Now, let's see if the model will fly," Picasso tells you. "It's already wound up."

Just then the band stops playing, and the dancing stops. The bandleader suddenly calls, "Shell out! Shell out!" as the waiters circulate among the tables and the dancers collect tips.

→ → → → → → → → → → → → →

Go on to the next page.

As the bandleader lifts his baton to start the music again, you press the lever on the side of the model plane. It takes off from your hands and soars skyward, circling the spinning ball of light over your head. Many of the customers applaud.

The plane heads back to the beaming Picasso. He reaches up and catches it in midflight as the band starts up again and the dancers resume their gyrations.

Just then, you notice a group of women and their escorts, big, heavyset guys, coming in the door of the cabaret.

Something about them makes you look twice. Maybe it's that they all look mad. Or maybe it's because they are pointing at your table.

Picasso is looking the other way, rewinding the rubber band of his plane. You tap him on the shoulder and point over at the door.

"Ah, a group of figure models has arrived," Picasso says.

"And they're coming over here," you say, exchanging nervous glances with Norman.

"You're right. I wonder what they want," Braque says, now having noticed them, too.

→ → → → → → → → → → → →

Go on to the next page.

"There they are!" one of the women shouts. "Braque and Picasso. They're the ones who have taken away our business. They don't paint *us* anymore, they just paint squares and circles. They've got all the other artists doing the same thing."

One of the boyfriends stands menacingly over Braque and Picasso. "What do you have to say for yourselves?" he growls.

Braque and Picasso stand up as the man flashes a knife.

"Hey!" Fernande cries. "They're serious about this."

We'd better get out of here fast," Norman whispers to you. "I think there's going to be a big fight."

Instinct tells you to make a dash for the door of the cabaret. On the other hand, you don't want to desert your new friends if they're in trouble.

You have to decide what to do fast. Several other mean-looking men are advancing on your table.

→ → → → → → → → → → → → →

If you make a dash for the door,
turn to page 99.
If you stay at your table, turn to page 75.

You decide to take the metro.

You and Miss Seymour have no trouble finding the right train and getting off at the correct stop, though Miss Seymour seems very nervous the whole way over.

The rest of the trip you make on foot. The sky is dark and leaden, and it's starting to rain.

"These stairs seem to go on forever," Miss Seymour says as you climb up the Butte. There are benches along the way, and Miss Seymour stops to rest every so often before you get to the top.

"This is a terrible neighborhood," she says, as you come to the vicinity of Picasso's studio. "These streets are nothing but muddy alleys."

"I know," you say. "But it's all the artists can afford."

As you get to the outside of the studio, you hear the sound of Braque's accordion. You can also hear a fiddle accompanying him.

You open the door to an incredible sight.

→ → → → → → → → → → → →

Turn to page 77.

It's broad daylight when you finally get back to the hotel but still very early in the morning. You've decided that if Miss Seymour is up, you'll tell her that you went out for an early morning walk—to see the sunrise over Paris. You just didn't want to disturb her, you'll explain.

As you enter the hotel, you see several French policemen standing near the front entrance. You'll skip the lift, you reason, and try to make it up the stairway to your room without being seen.

As you start up, you hear Miss Seymour's voice coming from the office of the concierge just off the downstairs hallway.

"You're trying to tell me that my student has *not* vanished?" Miss Seymour is saying.

"You say your student has vanished, Madame. I say that your student has not vanished," the concierge says.

"I am an expert on the kidnapping of children. I do not think this is a case of that. There is no note, no sign of struggle," another voice explains.

"That may be true, Inspector," Miss Seymour says. "But people do not just disappear."

"Perhaps if we search the building again," the inspector says.

"Good morning everyone," you say, walking casually into the office.

They all stand there in shock for a moment.

"You see. What did I tell you?" the inspector says. "All this fuss for nothing. Really, Madame."

"And what do you have to say for yourself?" Miss Seymour demands, her face flushed.

"I just went for an early morning walk, and—" you begin to explain.

"Preposterous," the concierge says. "You did not go past me. The front door rings a bell in my office if anyone opens it."

The inspector coughs politely. "Now that your problem is solved, you will excuse me," he says with a salute. He goes outside, where you see him through the window going off with the police.

"I don't know how you did it, and I don't want to know," Miss Seymour says as she takes you upstairs. "But I do know this. You are going to spend the day studying. And I am not letting you out of my sight."

"You're right," you say. "I really should catch up on my studies. In fact, I want to know everything there is to know about art. I want to know about every period and style."

"You do?" Miss Seymour says in amazement.

"I only ask one thing," you say.

"And what might that be?" Miss Seymour asks suspiciously.

"I want to go to Picasso's party tonight."

→ → → → → → → → → → → → →

Go on to the next page.

"Certainly not. He may be a good artist, but he's a bad influence," Miss Seymour says.

"How can you say that? You don't even know him," you protest.

"I know enough," Miss Seymour says.

"He even wants to do your portrait," you say.

"I'm sure he does. But I don't care to have my nose twisted or my eyes in the back of my head."

"But he can do a really realistic portrait when he wants to. You should see the 'Degas' he did at his studio."

"A Degas?"

"Yes, and Monsieur Degas himself will be at the party tonight," you say.

"He will? Degas will be there?"

"I'm sure of it," you say.

"All right, then. Finish your essay on French medieval history, and I'll think about going."

After dinner, Miss Seymour reads over the essay that you've spent all day writing.

"Not bad," she says. "We'll have your father read this over when he gets back."

"I worked really hard on it," you say.

"I can see that you did," Miss Seymour says.

"Then can we go to the party?" you ask.

"Well, perhaps we could stop by and meet Degas—but only for a short while," Miss Seymour says. "Do you know how to get to Picasso's studio?"

"We can take the metro for part of the way,"
you say.

"The metro? I'd rather not, this time of night,"
Miss Seymour says. "A taxi would be safer."

"I'm not sure I can give the right directions to
a taxi driver," you say. "I've forgotten the exact
address."

"I'm sure it will come to you," Miss Seymour
says. "I much prefer a taxi. However, if you feel
we *must* take the metro, then I guess we must."

← ← ← ← ← ← ← ← ← ← ← ←

If you decide to take the metro,
turn to page 69.

→ → → → → → → → → → → →

If you decide to take a taxi, turn to page 104.

You decide to stay at your table.

Braque suddenly gives the man with the knife a one-two combination punch to the side of the head. The knife falls to the floor as the man sinks to his knees, then falls over sideways. Picasso kicks the knife under the table with the side of his foot.

Three other men rush at your table. You take the tiny model plane and sail it at the head of the one in front. He ducks at the last moment, and the plane slams into the forehead of the man behind, knocking him backward. *His* head collides with the head of the third man, knocking them both out.

The models run for the door, screaming. The one escort left on his feet stops dead in his tracks, then backs off with his hands raised, turns, and runs for the door himself.

A number of people in the cabaret, including François and his son, stand and cheer as the bouncers carry off the unconscious bodies.

"I think I'd better be getting back to the hotel before Miss Seymour wakes up," you say.

"Don't forget about the party tomorrow," Fernande says.

"I'll try to make it," you say.

Norman leaves, too, and walks you to the metro. "See you at the party at nine," he says.

"I hope so," you say.

← ← ← ← ← ← ← ← ← ← ← ←

Turn to page 70.

Colored streamers and Chinese lanterns cover the ceiling. A large banner reading HONNEUR À ROUSSEAU has been hung on the wall. A figure you guess is Rousseau himself is seated on a kind of throne made with a chair on a low platform. He is playing a fiddle furiously.

About thirty people are crowded inside—mostly artists. Some are dressed as animals to honor Rousseau, whose "primitive" paintings are often of jungle scenes.

Fernande runs over when she sees you and Miss Seymour. "The two of you made it. I'm glad," she says. "Come to the back and try my paella while it lasts. Your friend Norman is already there, eating away."

"Is Monsieur Degas here?" Miss Seymour asks, looking around as Fernande leads the two of you to the food table.

"Not yet, but he will come. Pablo sent him a note apologizing for what he said this afternoon. And Degas has a great respect for Rousseau," Fernande says.

Norman greets you with his mouth full and hands you and Miss Seymour two plates of paella—rice mixed with seafood and chicken.

Suddenly the music stops, and everyone calls for Rousseau to give a speech.

→ → → → → → → → → → → → →

Go on to the next page.

"All right," Rousseau says, putting down his fiddle and getting to his feet. "Here's to the two greatest painters of our time—Picasso and Rousseau."

There is a round of applause.

"Gracias Rousseau," Picasso calls out in Spanish.

"You, Picasso, in the Egyptian style," Rousseau goes on, "and *I* in the modern style."

"I wonder what he means by that," you whisper to Norman.

"I'm not sure, but I think he means that Picasso's paintings are like the ones the ancient Egyptians did for their tombs," Norman says.

"Yes," you say. "I saw those in Egypt when I was younger. Picasso's paintings don't look much like them, however."

Rousseau sits down and begins playing his fiddle again. Several couples go back to dancing, though there is not much space to move in the crowded room.

Fernande pulls you and Miss Seymour through the crowd and over to a large, heavyset woman with a squarish head. "This is Gertrude Stein, a fellow American," Fernande says.

Gertrude is flanked by a much thinner woman on one side and a short, bald man on the other. You find out that one is her best friend, Alice B. Toklas, and the other is the art dealer Kahnweiler.

Suddenly there is a commotion at the front door of the studio. You notice it even over the din of the party. You look over and see Picasso and Braque greeting Degas.

"That's him, that's Degas," you tell Miss Seymour.

"I see him," she says. "This is so exciting."

Picasso brings Degas through the crowd, over to where you are standing. He is introduced all around. Miss Seymour looks as though she is going to faint.

"I'm so glad to see you, Monsieur Degas," Kahnweiler says. "I just bought one of your masterpieces. A pastel painting."

"You did?" Degas says. "Which one?"

"It's in the small storage room in the back that we're using for coats," Picasso says. "Come, I'll show you."

You, Norman, Braque, Fernande, and Miss Seymour follow them to the back of the studio.

"Here it is," Kahnweiler says, handing the painting to Degas.

Degas looks at it closely with his failing eyes. "I must have been tired when I did this," he says.

"In my humble opinion," Picasso says, "it's one of your best."

"It *is* quite remarkable, isn't it?" Degas says.

"Quite so," Kahnweiler says. "But I just noticed that you forgot to sign it."

→ → → → → → → → → → → →

Go on to the next page.

"I do that sometimes, I confess," Degas says. "But that's quickly remedied."

Picasso hands Degas a brush. Degas brings the painting close to his face and carefully signs it.

"Aha!" Picasso says. "I can paint in your style so well that even you can't tell your work from mine."

"What are you babbling about, Picasso?" Degas says.

"Yes, Pablo, what are you saying?" Kahnweiler asks.

"I did that painting, and Degas just signed it as if it were one of his own."

"Picasso is right. I saw him do the painting," Braque says.

"Of course you would say that. You're his best friend. Are we to believe you?" Degas says.

"These two will tell you. They saw me do it also," Picasso says, pointing to you and Norman.

You and Norman give each other a knowing look.

"I didn't see you do it," you say in a deadpan manner.

"I thought you told me you got it from a dealer," Norman says, playing along.

"Come on now, tell the truth," Picasso says.

"The truth is, it looks like a Degas and it's signed by Degas," Norman says.

Fernande starts to laugh.

"Monsieur Kahnweiler, would you like to buy this cubist sketch by Picasso?" you say, showing him Norman's sketch of the *Demoiselles*, the one Norman did and Picasso signed on your first visit to Picasso's studio.

"A cubist sketch! Why, I've been trying to get Pablo to sell me one since January. I'll give you five hundred francs for it."

"Only five hundred," Norman says. "I think it's a brilliant sketch."

"All right, eight hundred," Kahnweiler says.

"Wait a minute! I didn't do that," Picasso says.

"But it has your signature," you say.

"Who else could draw like this?" Norman says.

Picasso also starts to laugh. "I guess the joke's on me," he says.

"One thousand francs, no more," Kahnweiler says.

"Sold!" you say, with a triumphant handshake.

You have Kahnweiler give the money to Norman. Then Kahnweiler packs up the "Picasso" along with the "Degas" and goes off, very pleased with himself at having acquired two such great works of art.

"Thank you," Norman says. "My money for art supplies was getting low. You've made it possible for me to keep working."

"I'm glad that you intend to spend the money wisely," Miss Seymour says.

→ → → → → → → → → → →

Go on to the next page.

All of you go back to the studio where the party is still going on but now winding down. Fernande lets out a cry as she sees that the food table has been tipped over on its side and the remainder of the refreshments dumped on the floor. A number of the guests are helping to clean up the mess.

Rousseau, still on his thronelike chair, has fallen asleep and is leaning precariously to one side.

"Alice and I will take Monsieur Rousseau home," Gertrude Stein says. "That is if you can carry him to our carriage outside."

You, Norman, Braque, and Picasso step up on the low platform and gently pick up the sleeping Rousseau. You notice that his bald head is covered with wax that has dripped down from the lantern over his head.

"A fitting crown for the master of the miraculous," Picasso says, as you all carry Rousseau toward the door.

Outside, the four of you carry him to Gertrude's carriage and wave good-bye as it rumbles away down the bumpy street.

You turn around as Miss Seymour comes out of the studio with Degas. "I admire your work so much," she says to him. "I think you are truly the best artist here tonight."

→ → → → → → → → → → → →

Go on to the next page.

"Ah, Miss Seymour, you are a woman after my own heart," Degas says, shaking her hand warmly before hurrying off into the night.

Miss Seymour stands there for a moment as if thunderstruck. You have to shake her arm a couple of times to bring her back to reality.

You and Miss Seymour go back inside briefly, rejoin the others, and say good-night to Fernande and Picasso.

"It *was* a good party, wasn't it?" Fernande says.

"It certainly was," you say.

Then you, Miss Seymour, and Norman leave, starting back down the long hill toward the metro.

Miss Seymour has changed her mind once again about Norman. As of now, she thinks he is wonderful.

Together you spend the next few days seeing the sights of Paris—the Eiffel Tower, Notre-Dame, and the Arc de Triomphe. You, Miss Seymour, and Norman also go back to the Louvre several times.

After that, your parents return to Paris, and you get ready for your trip back home to the States.

On your last night in Paris, you have a farewell dinner—with Norman as the guest of honor.

Later, just before you go to bed, your father says, "I read your essay on French medieval history. It was good . . . as far as it went. But there are many points we should discuss in detail."

You groan inwardly. As much as you enjoyed your trip to Paris, you've had your fill of French history for the time being. It's going to be a long trip home.

The End

You decide to try to sneak out the front door of the hotel. As an afterthought, you carefully bundle up some of your clothes and arrange them under the covers of your bed. If Miss Seymour does look in on you during the night, you reason, it will look as though you are sleeping, especially in the dark.

You put on your jacket and take off your shoes. You can carry them while you sneak past Miss Seymour's room.

After turning off your oil lamp, you tiptoe down the hallway. The door to Miss Seymour's room is open slightly, but her room is dark.

You reach the end of the hallway and start down the stairs. Just then you hear voices on the stairway below. They are coming up toward you. You don't want to be seen, so you hurry back up the few steps you've already gone down and turn to go back to your room.

As luck would have it, the light goes on in Miss Seymour's room, spilling out into the hallway in front of you. You're trapped!

You notice the open lift a few feet back from the top of the stairway. It's dark inside and you can hide in there until the coast is clear, you decide. Silently, you slip inside and carefully close the door.

You listen on as the voices reach the top of the stairs and head down the hallway toward another room.

You wait awhile until all is quiet again, then try to open the door to the lift—but it's stuck! You try but you can't even locate the latch. You feel around in the darkness until you find something that could be the latch, and give it a pull.

Suddenly, with a whirring sound, the lift starts down. Maybe this will work out okay after all, you hope. You may be able to get off on the ground floor and just walk out the front door.

→ → → → → → → → → → → → →

Go on to the next page.

However, halfway down the lift comes to a sudden, jarring halt. You seem to be between floors. All is silent. In the dark, you try to find a button or a switch to start it up again. But no such luck.

As it turns out, the cable has jammed on the roof, and the cab is stuck in a spot where you can't get out. You'll be there for the rest of the night and half the next day—until the repairmen can get there and fix it. So much for your plan, you think.

But that's the least of your worries. Right now all that's on your mind is what Miss Seymour is going to say when you finally *do* get out.

The End

You decide to wait for Miss Seymour. Norman goes on ahead, but before he leaves he gives you detailed directions on how to get to Le Lapin Agile.

Miss Seymour comes back not long afterward. "I see that your friend Norman has left," she says. "Did you both enjoy your lunch?"

"The lunch was all right," you say. "But Norman told me about this great café where all the artists hang out. He left to go there. Can we go, too? He told me how to get there."

"Maybe," she says. "What's the name of this café?"

"It's called Le Lapin Agile."

"What an interesting name," Miss Seymour says. "The Agile Rabbit. I don't think I've ever heard of it."

"You'd certainly want to see a place with a name like that," you say.

"That may be true, but I know of a much more interesting place to go."

"Where's that?" you ask.

"Notre-Dame Cathedral," she says. "We can walk there along the river."

"I don't want to see a cathedral," you say.

"You'll like this one. It has hundreds of gargoyles and carvings of strange, birdlike creatures with beaked faces and huge claws."

"Really?" you say, getting a bit interested. "Well, okay. But I would still rather meet up with Norman."

"We'll find him later—sketching at the Louvre, I'm sure," Miss Seymour says.

You and Miss Seymour walk the short distance to the Seine and then up along the Left Bank toward the Île de la Cité. Soon you see the Cité up ahead, the twin towers of Notre-Dame reaching up into the sky.

"The island has been inhabited since prehistoric times," Miss Seymour says. "A tribe called the Parisii lived there."

"I guess that's where the name Paris came from," you say.

"I think you're right," Miss Seymour says. "It was later the site of a Roman encampment. And still later, the nucleus for the city of Paris."

You reach the bridge leading across to the Cité itself.

"This is called the Pont Neuf, or New Bridge," Miss Seymour says. "Even though it's one of the oldest in Paris."

"That makes sense," you say jokingly.

→ → → → → → → → → → → →
Go on to the next page.

You cross a square in front of the cathedral and go in through the main doorway. You spend the next two hours looking at the hundreds of large statues, beautiful stained-glass windows, the huge bell inside one of the towers, and especially the gargoyles on the upper balconies.

Miss Seymour was right: there's nothing like the gargoyles of Notre-Dame. They look like giant monsters perched to overlook Paris.

You go to the top of one of the towers, two hundred feet up, and take in the magnificent view of Paris. In front of you in the distance, the Eiffel Tower rises gracefully into the sky, and off to your right, you see the heights of Montmartre crowned with the sparkling white domed towers of the Church of Sacré-Coeur.

You stay in Paris for another week or so—until your parents come back from the south of France. You and Miss Seymour go to the Louvre several more times and make a few trips to other museums.

You never do meet up with your friend Norman Rockwell in Paris again, though in later years he is to become quite famous in the States.

→ → → → → → → → → → → →

Go on to the next page.

You learn a lot more about art and the city of Paris before you have to leave. You realize, though, that you've only begun to see all of the city. Perhaps one day you'll return and see the rest of it.

The End

You decide to go back to the café. Miss Seymour is probably waiting for you by now. You say good-bye to Norman and his friends and then run down to the Opéra and take the metro back.

"That lady?" the waiter says in thickly accented French. "You just missed her. Yes, I gave her the note. She paid the bill and left."

"Thanks," you call, as you run back toward the metro station. If she's heading for Le Lapin Agile, she might be taking the train, you determine. Maybe you can catch her before she gets on it.

You get to the platform just as a train pulls out. Fortunately, another train pulls into the station right behind it.

You jump on the train and sit down. After a short way, the train makes a sharp left turn. You don't remember that before!

You ask a woman sitting next to you if this is the right train for the Opéra. "*Mais non,*" she says. "This one goes to the Eiffel Tower. You can get off there and take a train back."

Oh, great, you think, now I'll never catch up with Miss Seymour.

The train soon arrives at the Eiffel Tower stop, and you get off. As you come out near the base of the tower, you look up in awe at the lacy superstructure soaring up into the sky.

→ → → → → → → → → → → →

Go on to the next page.

"It is magnificent, is it not?" an elderly man next to you says. "And to think it was considered ugly at the time it was built." The man notices your look of disbelief. "Oh, yes, they wanted to start tearing it down as soon as the World's Fair of 1889 was over. But fortunately the people managed to save it, and now we can see its true beauty. It's the world's tallest man-made structure, nine hundred and eighty-four feet high."

"You seem to know a lot about it," you say.

"Yes, I helped design and install its elevators," the man says. "Come, I'll get you in free. I have a pass. I ride to the top every day, sometimes several times a day, just to look out. I never get tired of the view."

You and the man go up the elevator in one of the pillars. After changing elevators twice, you reach the observation platform on top. You stand there in the wind, feeling as if you are a bird flying over the city. "You can see for forty miles in any direction from here," the man says.

You can hardly wait to get back and tell Miss Seymour about this. Oh, no! Miss Seymour! You'd forgotten that she's out there looking for you. She's probably frantic by now.

Before you head down, you stand back and take in the view one last time. For the time being, you'll just have to enjoy yourself while you can. You'll face the wrath of Miss Seymour later.

The End

You decide to go with your parents. The next morning you repack your things, and after saying good-bye to Miss Seymour for the time being, you board the taxi with your mother and father. At the railway station you get on the train going to the south of France.

You have nothing to complain about the train trip itself. The countryside is beautiful, and you can read or walk up and down the aisle as often as you like. The next day you arrive in a small, picturesque village in the south of France.

You have a large room all to yourself at an inn, with a view of the rolling hills around the town— some forested, some covered with grape orchards. The purple ridges of distant mountains rise behind them.

Your father is off somewhere most of the time, doing some kind of research, and your mother is with him. You are all right for a day or so, walking in the countryside, reading at night.

But before long things start to get boring. At least Miss Seymour made life kind of exciting, even if it wasn't always the way you liked it.

You try to grin and bear it until it's time to go back to Paris. But as hard as you try to amuse yourself, the time only passes more and more slowly. For now, you'll just have to think of something—anything—to fill your time. You hate to say it, but you really do miss Miss Seymour after all.

The End

You decide to run for it. You make a dash for the door with Norman right behind you. Just before you get outside, you glance back and see Braque punching one of the men. You also see two of them coming after you.

You and Norman start down one of the side streets leading off the square outside. The two men come out of the cabaret and run after you.

After running a few blocks, you and Norman stop for a moment. Both of you are breathing heavily.

"Those men chasing us can't be far behind," you say. "What'll we do?"

Norman looks around, then points across the street at the entrance to a graveyard. "Let's try to lose them in there," he says.

You run through a mossy, wrought iron gate and into the graveyard. Inside, the white tombstones and crypts shine eerily in the dim light.

→ → → → → → → → → → → → →

Go on to the next page.

You and Norman sprint down between the tombstones, then duck into a deep recess in the side of one of the crypts—just as the men chasing after you arrive panting at the entrance to the graveyard.

"No, wait!" you hear one of the men say as you crouch in the darkness.

"What is it?" the other one says.

"I . . . I don't like graveyards. They're haunted."

"Idiot! Coward! Come on or we'll lose them."

Suddenly you feel the cold fingers of a hand brush your neck. You let out a scream as you jump up in fright.

"What's the matter!" Norman gasps.

"It's a ghost!" you say.

"It's just the watchman," Norman says, looking behind you. There's a wine bottle in his hand. "I think you scared him—he's passed out."

"I'm sorry," you say. "I'll bet those men heard me."

"I'll bet they did, too," Norman says.

"I have an idea," you say. "Here, grab the watchman's black cape and his dark, floppy hat. Does he have any matches on him?"

"Uhh . . . yeah," Norman says, after looking through the man's pockets.

For the next few minutes, you and Norman work frantically. You punch eyeholes in part of your white shirt and practice sucking in part of the shirt to make a horrible-looking mouth.

"Okay, now," you say to Norman, and the two of you both start shouting. "Help! Keep away! Ahhhhhh!" you scream.

The two men are coming in your direction. Suddenly the first one stops dead in his tracks. His face turns ashen white.

→ → → → → → → → → → → →

Go on to the next page.

"Oh, for God's sake. What is it now?" the other man says.

Then he sees what the first man is looking at—a seven-foot-high ghost standing in the dark shadows of the crypt, its ghastly face lit by an eerie glow from under its chin. You and Norman shout even louder now.

Both of the men let out screams and streak in terror toward the entrance to the graveyard.

"You can get off my shoulders now," Norman says.

You climb down and take off the mask you made. You put the cape back over the sleeping watchman and replace his hat.

"That was great," Norman says excitedly.

"I'm just glad you didn't set me on fire with those matches," you say. Then you both nearly collapse laughing.

The two of you wait there in the darkness until you're sure the coast is clear. Then you carefully make your way out of the graveyard and back to the metro.

← ← ← ← ← ← ← ← ← ← ← ←

Turn to page 70.

You and Miss Seymour go down to the street in front of the hotel and start looking for a taxi. The sky is dark and leaden, and it's starting to rain. The street looks deserted in both directions.

"I guess we'll have to walk to one of the main boulevards," Miss Seymour says.

The rain starts to come down more heavily.

"I hope we can find a taxi soon, or we'll be drenched," you say.

Suddenly, a block ahead, you see a taxi pull up to the curb in front of a restaurant and let out a passenger.

"Wait here. I think I can catch that taxi," you say as you run toward it.

You reach the taxi just as it's about to pull away from the curb. The driver is sitting in a front compartment, a canvas canopy over his head.

"Are you available?" you ask.

"Most certainly," the driver says. He gets out of the taxi and opens the door of the passenger compartment for you.

"We need to pick up Miss Seymour, my tutor, in the next block," you say as you get in.

You manage to get Miss Seymour in the taxi just before the heavens open up and the rain descends in a terrific downpour.

The driver slides open the panel between the front and passenger compartments. "Where to?" he asks.

"Montmartre," you say.

"Montmartre?" the driver repeats. "In this downpour? It would be very risky. The roads up there turn into muddy streams in this kind of weather."

"I'm sure that this is just a passing shower," Miss Seymour says.

"Well, I'll give it a try. But what is the address?" the driver says.

"I'm not sure," you say. "But I think I can find it."

"That would be impossible," the driver says. "Montmartre is a maze of narrow, twisting streets, especially in this weather. You will have to find some other way of getting there."

"No, wait a minute," you say, "I just remembered. It's thirteen Rue Ravignan."

"A very bad address," the driver says. "A neighborhood infested with thieves and vagabonds."

"And artists," you say.

→ → → → → → → → → → → → →

Go on to the next page.

"The so-called artists are hardly better than the other riffraff that hangs out there," the driver says.

"I think we'd better get out and—" you start.

"No, no. I'll take you there. It is my duty," the driver says.

The taxi starts off down the street, its motor putt-putting with an occasional coughlike back-fire. It splashes through a number of deep puddles.

The rain is already dying down, and the wet streets glisten with the reflections of the street-lamps. You go across a bridge over the Seine— the river now veiled in mist.

"This looks like an impressionist painting," you say, looking though the window. "Everything is fuzzy."

"Yes, you are quite right," Miss Seymour says, pleased by your observation.

Fifteen minutes later, the rain has stopped, and you come to the base of a steep hill. The driver starts up without hesitation.

Partway up, the taxi slows to a crawl, as the motor struggles to get up the hill.

"The road is very slippery because of the rain," the driver says, "I'm not sure we can make it to the top."

Then the taxi comes to a stop and starts to slide slowly backward.

"Mon Dieu!" the driver exclaims, madly pressing down on the brake pedal. "My God! I think the water that spashed up under us has finished our brakes!"

You and Miss Seymour look with horror out the back window as the taxi begins to pick up speed—sliding backward down the hill. Somehow the driver manages to steer so that you don't go off the road or hit anything on the way down.

→ → → → → → → → → → → →

Go on to the next page.

At the bottom of the hill, the road levels off. The taxi spins around as the driver straightens it out. It slows but keeps going. As luck would have it, a streetcar is coming along the middle of the avenue at the same time. The taxi, now moving rather slowly, nevertheless slides into the side of the streetcar with a resounding thud.

You and Miss Seymour are jolted and thrown forward against the front partition of the cab. Fortunately neither of you is hurt.

The streetcar driver, the conductor, and a number of the passengers come dashing out and around to where the taxi hit. The taxi driver jumps out and immediately launches into a shouting match with the streetcar conductor. Soon they are trading punches, with the streetcar passengers crowded around, cheering on the conductor.

You and Miss Seymour are getting out of the taxi just as the shrill sound of a whistle pierces the air behind you. A policeman strides up to the scene, at the same time taking out a small notebook.

The conductor and the taxi driver stop fighting and immediately start trying to tell the officer their side of the story—both at the same time. The policeman quiets them down.

→ → → → → → → → → → → → →

Go on to the next page.

"You must come to the station," the policeman says. "I need a statement from everyone here. I must file a complete report—in triplicate."

You never do get to Rousseau's party. You and Miss Seymour are at the station for hours while dozens of statements are carefully taken. The police are very impressed with your grasp of the French language, something unusual for Americans.

Later, they have a horse-drawn carriage take you and Miss Seymour back to the hotel.

Unfortunately, you don't get to see Norman and your other Parisian friends again, at least for the time being. Miss Seymour keeps a close watch on you until your parents come back from the south of France and you start on your trip back to the States.

Somehow though, you know you will get back to Paris one of these days. And you can hardly wait for the chance to go off on your own and *really* see the city.

The End

Glossary

Bateau-Lavoir ("Laundry Boat"), No. 13, Rue Ravignan—The building in the Montmartre
section of Paris where many artists had their
studios in the early part of this century. The
building started out as a piano factory, became a locksmith's workshop, and was finally converted by the owner into studios.
Picasso had his studio here from 1904 to 1909
on the ground floor in the back, looking out
on Rue Garreau. The building got the nickname "Bateau-Lavoir" because with all the
laundry usually hanging outside, it resem-
bled one of the laundry boats moored in the
Seine. It was a ramshackle, multistoried
building clinging to the side of a hill that
appeared to be a single-story building from
the main entrance on Rue Ravignan.

Braque, Georges (1882–1963)—In his early career
as an artist, Braque was one of the fauvists
(see page 112). Later he became a close
friend of Picasso for many years, exchanging ideas with him on a daily basis. Together they developed the cubist style,
painting mostly still lifes.

Champs-Élysées ("Elysian fields")—The most famous avenue of Paris. It is lined with gardens and rows of chestnut trees. A grand
arch, the Arc de Triomphe built by the em-
peror Napoleon, stands at its western end.

Cubism—A style created by the painters Braque and Picasso between 1907 and 1909. It emphasized the flat, two-dimensional surface of the canvas or drawing paper and rejected the traditional techniques of perspective and shading. The name is said to have come from a remark by Matisse, who thought the paintings looked as if they were made up of cubes.

Degas, Edgar (1834–1917)—A French painter and sculptor known for the soft and luminous color of his paintings, as well as their sense of movement and spontaneity. Degas suffered from eye trouble as the result of an injury he received in the Franco-Prussian war of 1870–71, where he served as a captain.

Eiffel Tower—The tall, pointed tower and chief Parisian landmark constructed with seven thousand tons of iron and steel. It was designed by Alexandre Gustave Eiffel for the international exposition of 1889. It rises to 984 feet from a base 330 feet square. For many years it was the highest man-made structure in the world, more than twice as high as the pyramid of Khufu in Egypt. Today the Empire State Building in New York City is much taller, at 1,472 feet.

Fauvists ("Wild beasts")—A group of artists (especially from 1898 to 1908) who used pure, brilliant color, usually applied directly from the paint tube. Shocked critics called the fauvists "wild beasts" from the violence of their color and their "shocking" and aggressive way of painting. Matisse was the leader of the movement, though he was later also influenced by cubism.

Impressionism—An art movement, mainly in France, in the late nineteenth and early twentieth centuries. The impressionist artists attempted to record visual reality in terms of the effects of light and color on the eye.

Louvre Museum—One of the largest museums in the world, the Louvre covers forty acres on the Right (north) Bank of the Seine River in Paris. The first Louvre building was built as a fort around the year 1200. Later it was expanded and became a royal residence. The main portion was built by King Louis XIV (1638–1715). After the French Revolution, the Louvre was made into a museum and today boasts eight miles of galleries showing works from virtually every period of art.

Matisse, Henri (1869–1954)—A very influential painter. The leader of the fauvists, Matisse used intense color and spontaneous lines to produce a sense of rhythm and movement, often using unusual color combinations and elaborate patterns. From 1907 on, he was influenced by the cubists and also did many pieces of sculpture.

Notre-Dame Cathedral—This famous "Gothic style" cathedral is on the Île de la Cité, a small island in the heart of Paris. It was begun in 1163 and completed 180 years later in 1313.

Paris—The capital of and largest city in France. Paris is famous for its palaces, gardens, and parks. At night, its buildings and monuments, including the Eiffel Tower, are lit up, giving Paris the nickname of the "city of light." Originally, Paris was a Roman colony on the Île de la Cité, an island in the Seine. During the Middle Ages, it spread to both banks and gradually grew into the Paris of today.

Picasso, Pablo (1881–1973)—Born in Málaga, Spain, Picasso became one of the most influential artists of the twentieth century. He showed his outstanding artistic ability by the age of ten. In 1895, when Picasso was fourteen, his family moved to Barcelona where he entered the local art academy. After several visits to Paris, Picasso moved there permanently in 1904. Between 1908 and 1912, Picasso and his friend Georges Braque worked together to launch the new movement of cubism (see page 112).

Rockwell, Norman (1894–1978)—An American artist and illustrator born in New York City, best known for his folksy covers for the magazine *The Saturday Evening Post*. Rockwell was a professional artist by the age of sixteen. A careful draftsman, he realistically depicted people from everyday life—usually with a touch of humor.

Rousseau, Henri (1844–1910). Also called *Le Douanier* ("Customs official")—Rousseau painted richly colored and carefully detailed scenes, usually of (imagined) lush jungles, in a simple, childlike manner (often termed "primitive"). His paintings went unnoticed for many years, and Rousseau made his living as a customs official. In 1893, he retired from the tollhouse where he worked to devote himself entirely to painting. He was soon "discovered" by young avant-garde painters like Picasso and Braque. In 1908, Picasso organized a banquet in Rousseau's honor to which all the leading artists and critics were invited.

Stein, Gertrude (1874–1946)—An American author who lived in Paris as an expatriate with her brother, Leo. Their apartment at 27 Rue de Fleurs became famous as a "salon," a gathering place for the painters, poets, and writers of the period.

Toklas, Alice B. (1878–1967)—An American author who was best known as the companion and confidant of Gertrude Stein, a relationship that lasted for forty years from 1907 to Stein's death in 1946. It was only after Stein's death that Toklas became a celebrity in her own right with the publication of her memoirs and two cookbooks.

Suggested Reading

If you enjoyed this book, here are some other books on Paris and art that you might like:

Boggs, Jean Sutherland. *Degas.* New York: Metropolitan Museum of Art, 1988. This is a catalog of the first large-scale exhibition of Degas's works, covering his oil paintings, charcoal and pencil drawings, pastels, and sculpture. All 392 works in the exhibition are fully illustrated. There is a full-page color illustration of his *Absinthe Drinker,* also called *In a Café.* A final chapter is included on his later years, when despite his failing eyesight, he never stopped working.

Gaunt, William. *Impressionism, A Visual History.* New York: Praeger Publishing, 1970. After a short and easy-to-read introduction describing the aims and achievements of the impressionists, this book contains a magnificent series of color plates. Each plate is accompanied by an analysis of the painting shown.

Huffington, Arianna Stassinopoulos. *Picasso, Creator and Destroyer.* New York: Simon &

Schuster, 1988. This landmark biography brings Picasso to full, magnificent life. Based on five years of research and interviews, it analyzes the complex relationships between Picasso and other creative "geniuses" of the time, such as Matisse, Braque, and Gertrude Stein.

Morariu, Modest. *Douanier Rousseau*. London: Murrays, 1975. A European publication that nevertheless seems to be well distributed in the United States. This is basically a large picture book of black and white and color plates. It has a brief text giving a concise history and interpretation of the artist. It is one of a series of books that include volumes on Picasso, Gauguin, impressionism, and many other related terms and figures.

O'Brian, Patrick. *Picasso*. New York: G. P. Putnam's Sons, 1976. This biography of Picasso traces his life from his birth in Spain on October 25, 1881 through his childhood, his early career in Spain, his bohemian days in Paris, and his later years. It gives a good coverage of the development of cubism and tries to explain Picasso's extraordinary talent.

Raynal, Maurice. *Picasso*. New York: Crown Publications, 1973. Although small in size, this book gives a very good critique of Picasso's work and includes sixty "tipped-in" color plates of excellent quality. It is one volume of a series that covers Braque, Degas, Matisse, and many others.

Rockwell, Norman. *My Adventures as an Illustrator*. New York: Doubleday, 1960. This very readable and fascinating autobiography follows the artist's life from early childhood through adolescence to his adult years. It is filled with excitement and humor as he relates with considerable wit his successes and failures as an artist.

Russell, John. *Paris*. New York: Harry N. Abrams, 1983. This is a spectacular book on Paris. It is lavishly illustrated and produced, with a well-written text, and illustrated by 310 paintings, pastels, drawings, and photographs, 85 of them in full color.

ABOUT THE AUTHOR

RICHARD BRIGHTFIELD is a graduate of Johns Hopkins University, where he studied biology, psychology, and archaeology. For many years he worked as a graphic designer at Columbia University. He has written many books in the Choose Your Own Adventure series, including *Master of Tae Kwon Do, Hijacked!, Master of Karate*, and *Master of Martial Arts*. In addition, Mr. Brightfield is the author of the first three books in The Young Indiana Jones Chronicles series. He has also coauthored more than a dozen game books with his wife, Glory. The Brightfields and their daughter, Savitri, now live on the coast of southern Florida.

ABOUT THE ILLUSTRATOR

FRANK BOLLE studied at Pratt Institute. He has worked as an illustrator for many national magazines and now creates and draws cartoons for magazines as well. He has also worked in advertising and children's educational materials and has drawn and collaborated on several newspaper comic strips, including *Annie* and *Winnie Winkle*. He has illustrated many books in the Choose Your Own Adventure series, most recently *Daredevil Park, Kidnapped!, The Terrorist Trap, Ghost Train, Magic Master*, and *Master of Martial Arts*. He is also the illustrator of the first three books in The Young Indiana Jones Chronicles series. A native of Brooklyn Heights, New York, Mr. Bolle now lives and works in Westport, Connecticut.

The name that means adventure —
INDIANA JONES!

THE YOUNG

INDIANA JONES™

CHRONICLES

CHOOSE YOUR OWN ADVENTURE ®

☐ **THE VALLEY OF THE KING**
The Young Indiana Jones Chronicles #1
$3.25/$3.99 in Canada   29756-2

☐ **SOUTH OF THE BORDER**
The Young Indiana Jones Chronicles #2
$3.25/$3.99 in Canada   29757-0

☐ **REVOLUTION IN RUSSIA**
The Young Indiana Jones Chronicles #3
$3.25/$3.99 in Canada   29784-8

☐ **MASTERS OF THE LOUVRE**
The Yong Indiana Jones Chronicles #4
$3.25/$3.99 in Canada   29969-7

**Straight from
George Lucas'
thrilling TV
series The
Young Indiana
Jones
Chronicles—
terrific
adventure
stories that let
YOU be young
Indiana Jones!**